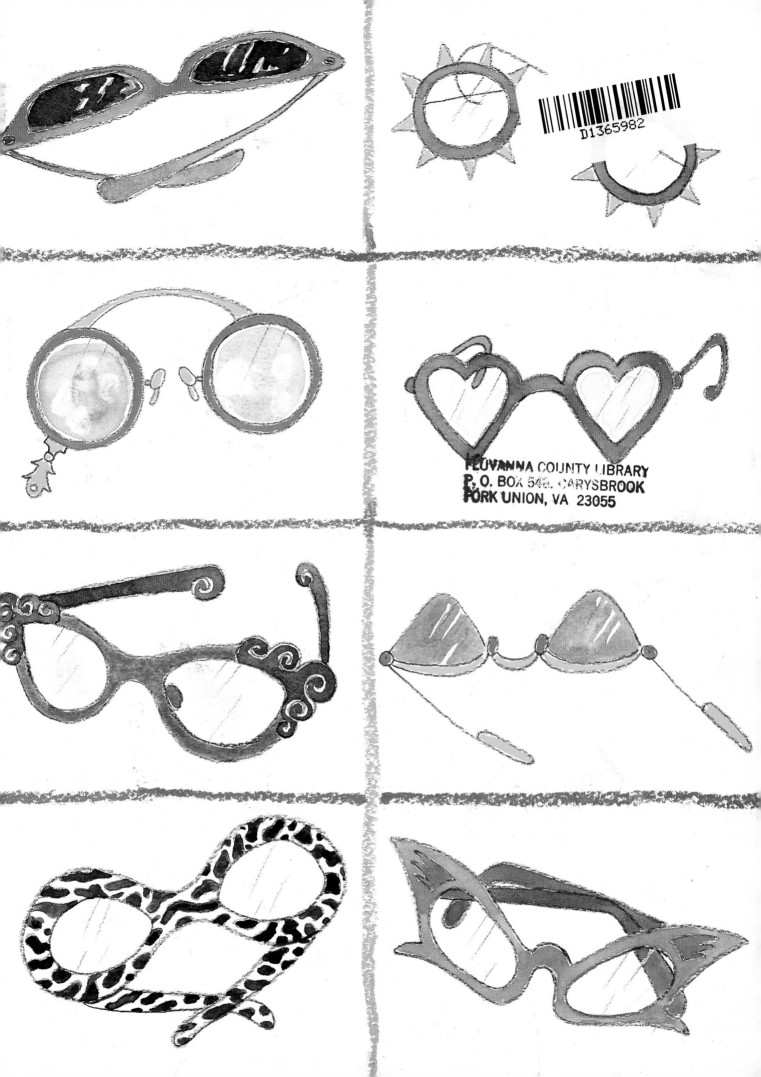

FLUVANNA COUNTY LIBRARY
P. O. BOX 548, CARYSBROOK
FORK UNION, VA 23055

D1365982

For Mom and Dad

- *miss you*

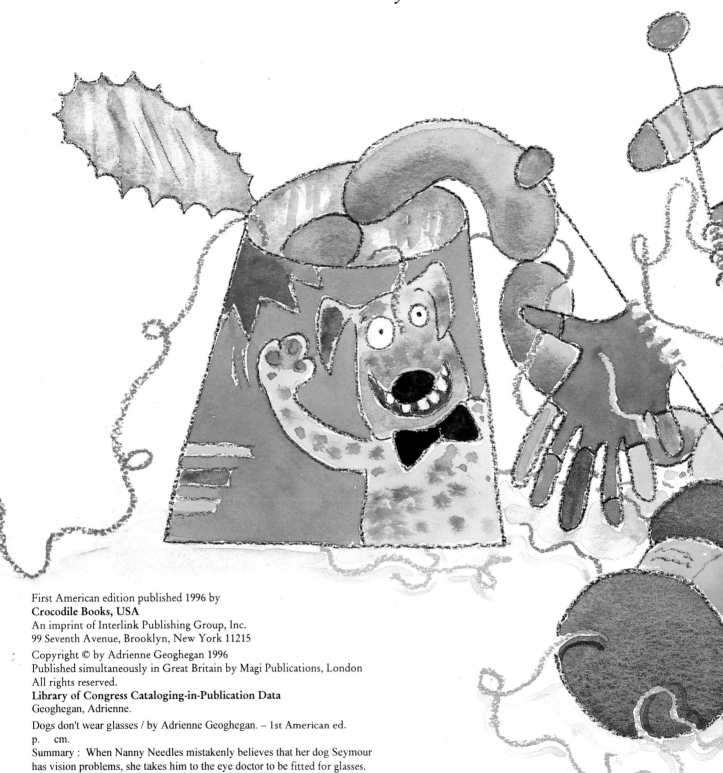

First American edition published 1996 by
Crocodile Books, USA
An imprint of Interlink Publishing Group, Inc.
99 Seventh Avenue, Brooklyn, New York 11215

Copyright © by Adrienne Geoghegan 1996
Published simultaneously in Great Britain by Magi Publications, London
All rights reserved.
Library of Congress Cataloging-in-Publication Data
Geoghegan, Adrienne.

Dogs don't wear glasses / by Adrienne Geoghegan. – 1st American ed.
p. cm.
Summary : When Nanny Needles mistakenly believes that her dog Seymour
has vision problems, she takes him to the eye doctor to be fitted for glasses.
ISBN 1-56656-208-2 (HB)

[1. Dogs–Fiction. 2. Vision–Fiction. 3. Humorous stories.]
I. Title.

PZ7 . G2927Do 1996 [E] – dc20 95 – 21910 CIP AC
Printed and bound in Italy
10 9 8 7 6 5 4 3 2 1

96-301
E
GEO

FLUVANNA COUNTY LIBRARY
P. O. BOX 548, CARYSBROOK
FORK UNION, VA 23055

Dogs Don't Wear Glasses

by

ADRIENNE GEOGHEGAN

Crocodile Books, USA

An imprint of Interlink Publishing Group, Inc.
NEW YORK

Nanny Needles spent most of her time in bed knitting sweaters.

Seymour, her dog, was perfectly happy with this arrangement.

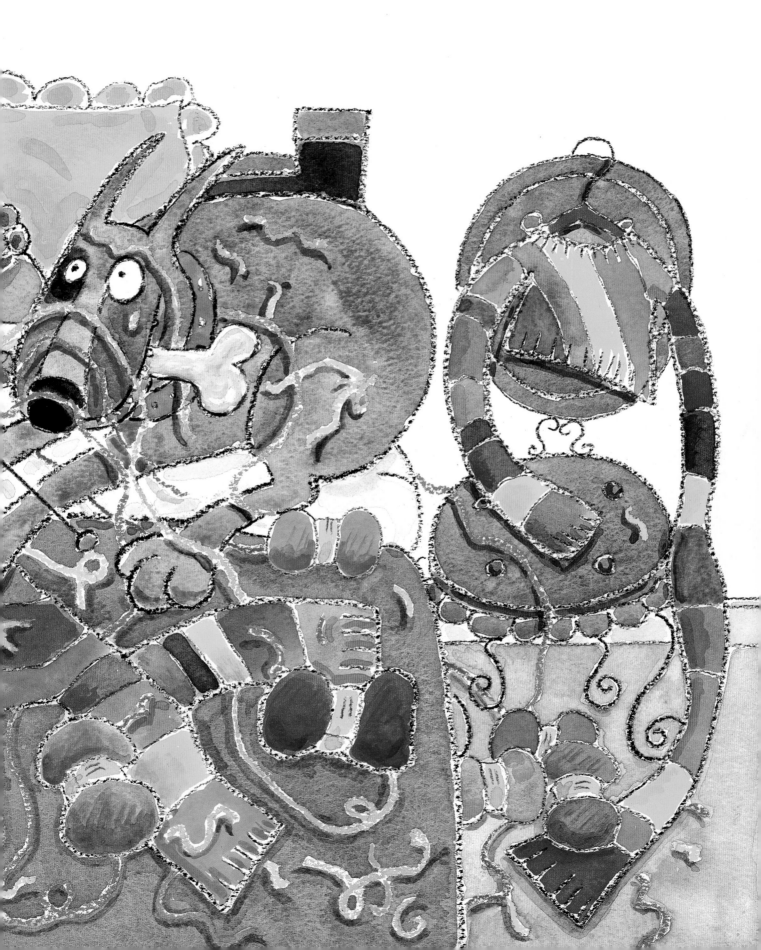

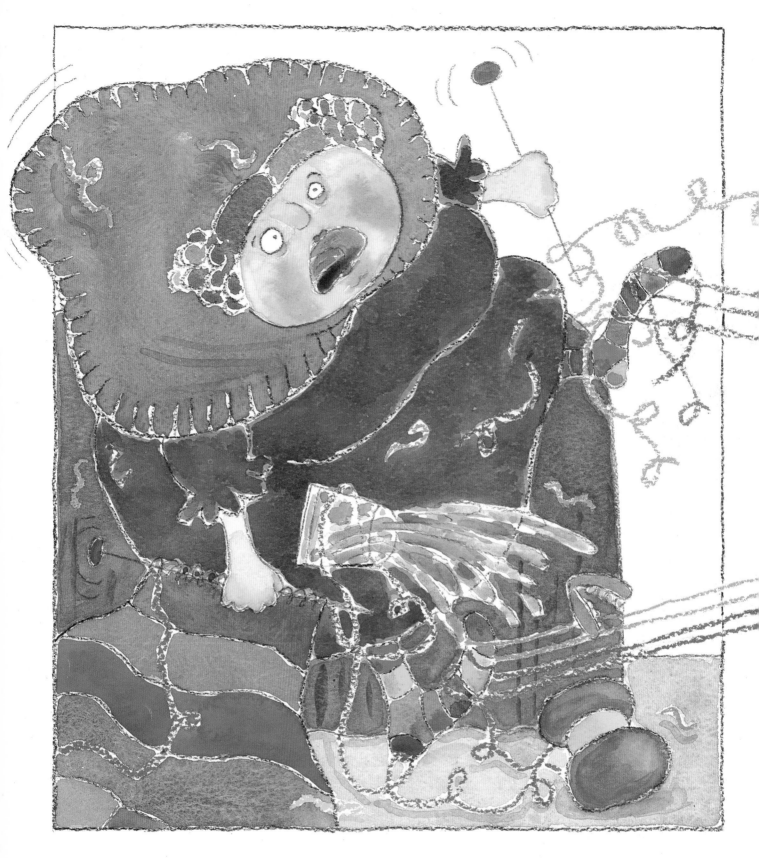

One day Nanny Needles was feeling rather lively,
so she hopped out of bed. As she did, her wool got
tangled up with Seymour's bone.

"You crazy dog!" she shouted. "Don't bring that
filthy bone into bed again!"
Seymour growled a little growl and ran off into the
kitchen to keep out of Nanny's way.

But Nanny Needles got there first.
She began to sweep the floor. She scrubbed
and she swept and she shined. She started
to pour the trash into the can –

SPLASH! SPLATTER!
SPLAT!

She missed!
The whole mess landed on Seymour's head.
He licked off the good parts.
"You clumsy dog!" she scolded. "You must watch
where you sit. Perhaps you need your eyes tested."

Seymour crept over to his bed, next to Nanny Needles' laundry basket, and hid his bone under the blankets.

"I think I'll do my washing now while that dog is out from under my feet," said Nanny Needles.

To Seymour's horror, Nanny Needles threw all *his*
things into the washing machine – his bone, his blanket,
his pillow, and his chewed-up slipper.

They all spun around and around in the warm sudsy
water. After the machine stopped, Nanny Needles
opened it to remove her laundry . . .

. . . but all she found was a teeny-weeny bone, a handkerchief blanket, a pincushion pillow, and one chewed-up little slipper.

"This is *your* stuff, Seymour," she shouted. "Where's *my* laundry?"

Nanny Needles felt exhausted.

"Oh, Seymour, whatever will I do with you?" she cried. "Perhaps your hair is getting in your eyes. I know! I'll give you a haircut."

But she cut too much off the top of Seymour's
head and left him with a large pink bald spot.

Seymour ran off and hid under the bed
for a nice quiet nap. He woke up to the
sound of the can opener.
"Mm, dinner," he thought. But to his amazement,
Nanny Needles gave him . . .

. . . sausages, peas, and French fries on a china plate.
Then she sat down and ate a bowl of Beef and Liver
for Healthy Dogs.

Afterwards, she felt a bit queasy.
When she had recovered, she looked at her empty bowl.
"Oh, no! What have I eaten?" she cried. *"And where are
my sausages?"*

Seymour was hiding under Nanny Needles' bed again.

"Have you eaten my sausages?" cried Nanny Needles.
"I'm not blaming you. It must be your eyes. I think
you need them tested so you can see more, Seymour."

The next day they were off to the eye doctor's.

"Sorry," said Mr. Lensman. "Dogs don't wear glasses."
"But he can't see a thing!" said Nanny Needles.
"He bumps into everything, and he eats my sausages
and mixes up my laundry and . . . and . . ."
"*All right, all right,*" said Mr. Lensman. "He can have
an eye test."

The eye test went perfectly, but Nanny Needles
still insisted that Seymour needed glasses.

"Try these," said Mr. Lensman.
Seymour felt seasick.

"What about these nice modern
mauve ones?" asked Nanny Needles.
But when Seymour looked through
them, everyone seemed to get very
skinny and almost disappear.

"Ooh, I like those green tinted ones,"
said Nanny Needles. Seymour looked
into the mirror, but he appeared a
little bit froggy!

"These blue ones are on sale," said Mr. Lensman.
Seymour didn't like them. They clashed with his pink scalp.
Nanny Needles felt differently.
"Oh, Seymour," she cried. "What lovely blue frames. They
really do suit your coloring." Before Seymour could protest,
Nanny Needles had bought them.

"Now put them on," said Nanny Needles, when they arrived home.

But Seymour refused to wear them.

"Would you like me to try them on first?" she coaxed.

"Then you can see how smart they look."

So Nanny Needles tried them on and looked in the mirror.

"My goodness!" cried Nanny Needles. "Everything
looks so big and bright and wonderful!"
Then she looked at Seymour.

"Why, Seymour," she said. "You've grown quite
bald and fat in your old age. Perhaps you need
to go on a *diet*!"

Dogs don't wear glasses
Geoghegan, Adrienne

47174
E GEO

Disard

Fluvanna County Library

E
GEO

96-301

Geoghegan, Adrienne

Dogs don't wear
glasses

$14.95

DATE			

FLUVANNA COUNTY LIBRARY
P. O. BOX 548, CARYSBROOK
FORK UNION, VA 23055

Borrowers Are Responsible
For Lost Or Damaged Materials

BAKER & TAYLOR

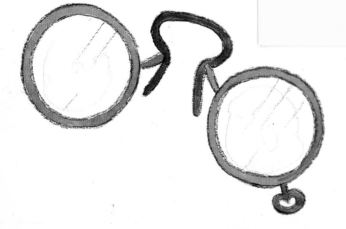

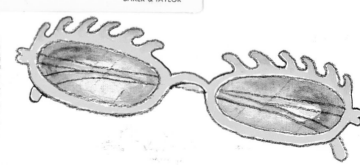